MADDIE'S MONSTER DAD

written and illustrated by

Scott Gibala-Broxholm

GODZILLA
GREEN

Marshall Cavendish Children

Marshall Cavendish Corporation
99 White Plains Road
Tarrytown, NY 10591
www.marshallcavendish.us/kids

Library of Congress Cataloging-in-Publication Data
Gibala-Broxholm, Scott.
Maddie's monster dad / written and illustrated by Scott Gibala-Broxholm.
— 1st ed.   p. cm.
Summary: Maddie loves it when her father plays scary games with her,
but when he is too busy with work she turns into a "Maddie Scientist" and builds herself a monster dad that she thinks will be more fun.
ISBN 978-0-7614-5846-3 (hardcover)   ISBN 978-0-7614-6008-4 (ebook)
[1. Fathers and daughters—Fiction. 2. Monsters—Fiction.] I. Title.
PZ7.G339095Mad 2011   [E]—dc22   2010013270

The illustrations were ghoulishly rendered in gouache and pencil.
Book design by Anahid Hamparian
Editor: Robin Benjamin

Printed in China (E)
First edition
10 9 8 7 6 5 4 3 2 1
mc Marshall Cavendish
Children

For the love of my life, Janice.
Dr. Frankenstein could not create
a more perfect soul mate for me than you!
And
for Boris Karloff,
the kindest
"monster" of them all!

Maddie LOVED monsters very scary much.
Her favorite color was Godzilla Green.

She ate Creature Crunchies for breakfast every day,

and Hide-and-**EEK** was her favorite game.

She wore werewolf sneakers that glowed in the dark.
When she stomped her feet, they even howled and growled.

Maddie LOVED playing with her dad, too.
He would swing her around like a flying saucer.

He baked cookies shaped just like the Glob from the Lake.

And he drew the most wonderful pictures . . .

. . . like a cat with HUGE fangs and bat wings!

...ut lately, her dad was VERY busy working from morning till night.

"Daddy, will you show me how to draw an alien with three arms and four legs and five . . . million, gazillion eyeballs?"

"I'll show you later, Maddie," he said. "As soon as I finish my work."
But when "later" arrived, he was too busy to draw it for her.

On Maddie's birthday, her father gave her a Build-a-Beast kit. "Daddy, will you help me make a creepy, kooky, spooky, scary, hairy, horrible, terrible, monstrous monster?" she asked.

"When I'm done," he told her.
But he was never "done."

Maddie plopped down in her favorite chair to watch her favorite movie: Curse of the Ghost of the Brain of the Bride of the Son of the Daughter of Frankenstein . . . 2.

"Daddy, will you watch it with me . . . PLEEEEASE?"

"I will later," he said. "I still have work to do."

Maddie's sneakers growled. She was MAD!

The sky grew cloudy and dark. A storm was heading their way.

"I'm going to make a new dad!"
the Maddie Scientist howled.
She opened up the Build-a-Beast kit.
Lightning flashed and thunder rumbled.
She colored and taped,
and stapled and taped,
and glued and taped
some more.

Then Maddie cut out lightning bolts.
"Now I'll make him come to life!"
She clapped her hands together.
There was a FLASH of light.

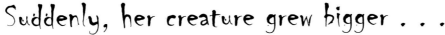

Suddenly, her creature grew bigger . . .

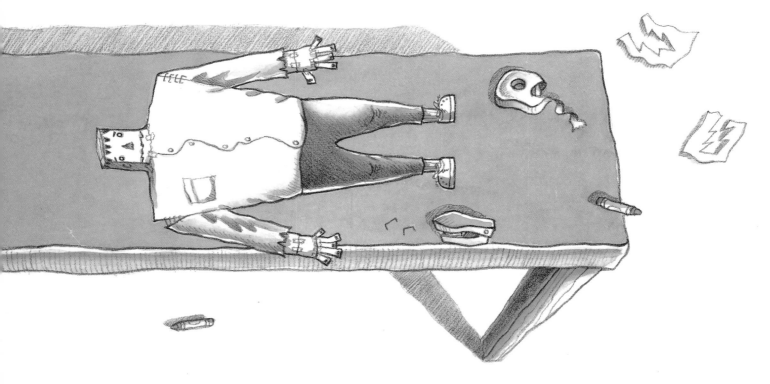

and bigger . . .

and BIGGER . . .

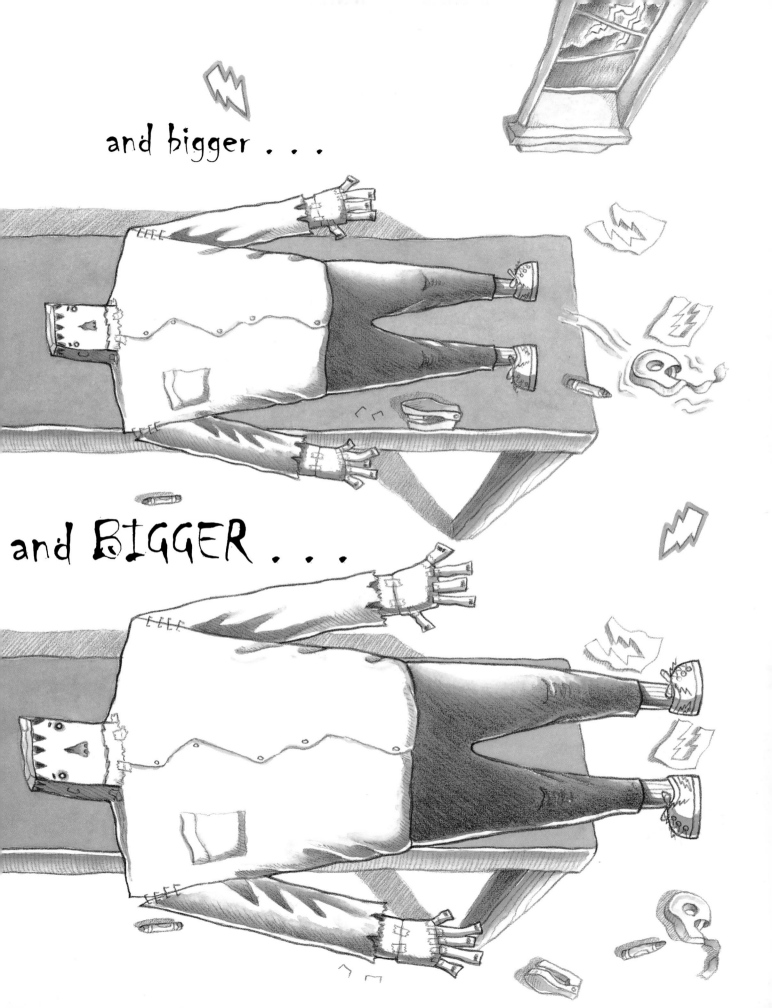

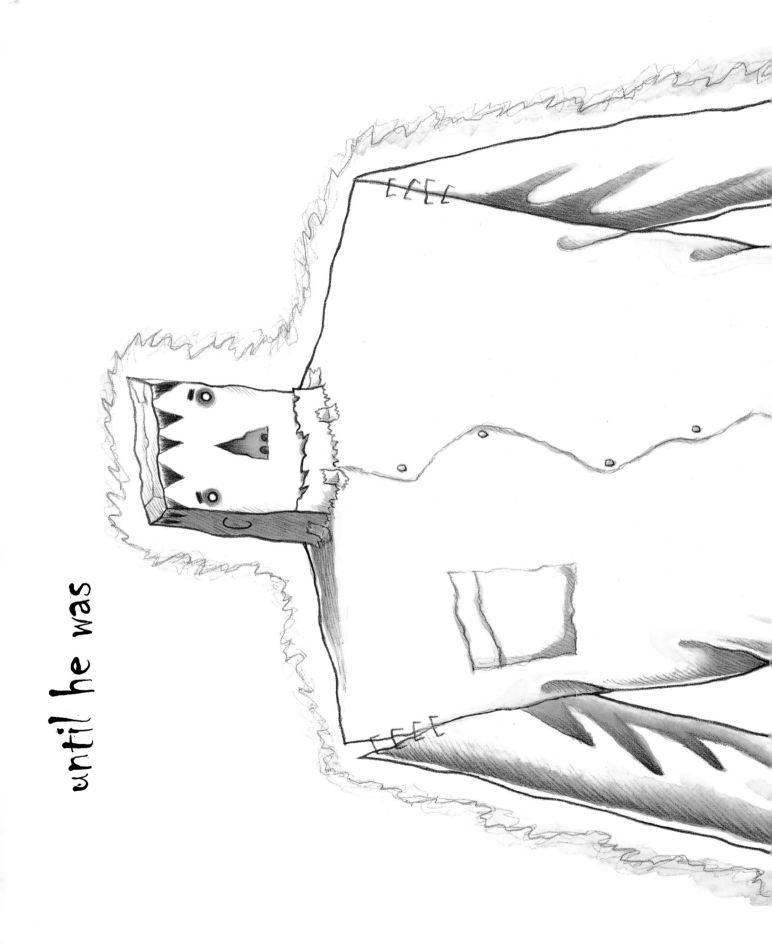

until he was

"My Monster Dad's ALIVE!" Maddie shrieked.
She gave him a VERY HIGH high-five.
"Let's play!"

First, they tried a game of Hide-and-EEK.
But the Monster Dad was just too easy
to find.

He swung her around like a flying saucer—
whirling and twirling and swirling through space.
It made her WAAAAY too dizzy!

For a snack, they tried to make Glob cookies.
But they were more like Glob rocks.

Then the Monster Dad drew a picture for her:
the creepiest, spookiest, scariest . . .

scribble.

Finally, they ran out of things to do. Maddie sighed.
"Now what?"

"**I KNOW!**
Let's scare my real dad!"

So they grabbed all the toilet paper they could find.

They wrapped each other up and pretended

to be mummies from a long time ago.

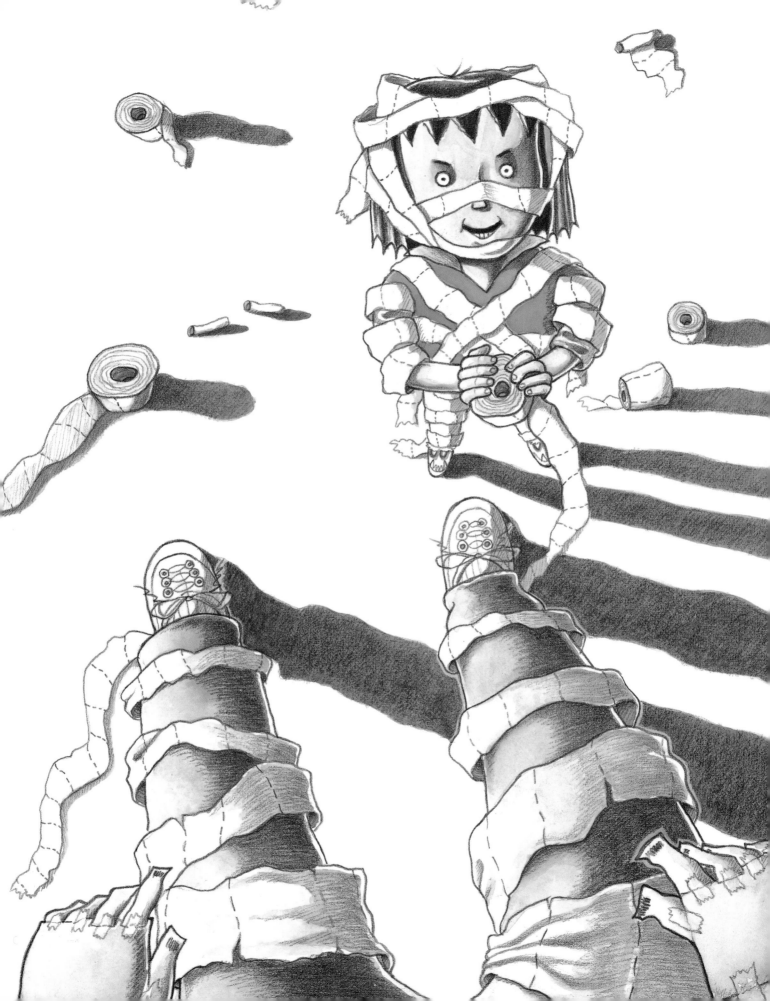

Slowly, they dragged their mummy feet
across the squeaky floor . . .
up the winding staircase . . .

and
down
the
LONG,
dark
hallway
to her dad's office.

Maddie tapped her dad on the shoulder.
"What are you doing, Daddy?"

"I'm finishing up the illustrations for a new monster book." He dad looked tired. "What are YOU doing?"
"I made a Monster Dad. We're mummies coming to scare you!

"You do look VERRRY scary!"
he agreed with a smile.

Maddie looked at
the Monster Dad.

Suddenly

he was

a toy

again.

"You know what?" her dad said. "I should really take a break. How would you like to make Glob cookies with me?"

Maddie was SO excited that she gave her dad a great big **MONSTER** hug!

He swung her around
like a ghost floating on air.

Her werewolf sneakers **HOWLED** with delight.

When the cookies were done, they played Hide-and-EEK.
After that, they drew an alien that was out of this world.

Later on . . .

"Daddy, can we get a puppy?" asked Maddie.
"Not right now, sweetie," he said.
"Hmmmm." She opened the
Build-a-Beast kit. . . .